NAKED

A Rhythmic Expression

Tim Duncan

Contents

Giving Me 4

Last Time I Checked 5

Sprinkle 7

It Ain't Heavy 8

Reflection 10

The Soul of A Man 12

She Arrived 13

Rose Petals 15

The little things... 17

Me Myself and I 19

Babe... 21

Heads or Tails... 22

Can You?... 23

Addiction... 24

Does she still exist?...................................... 25

A Couple of Forever's are Not Needed................ 27

Silent Night... 28

Extension of Goodness 29

Wild Thoughts.. 31

Because she could 32

Just want you to KNOW................................. 34

Need You vs Want You!....................36

From My View Point.....................38

Be You!.....................40

It's Funny.....................41

Would you mind if.....................42

Get Out of My Head.....................44

Love Me Thoughts 45

Have you ever.....................46

Brush Stokes 47

Your smile 48

The Taste of Cognac 49

Selfless.....................51

Infinity 52

Dream Chaser.....................54

Climax.....................55

Open Your Eyes 56

Facts 57

You!.....................59

I met this woman 60

My Love.....................61

Ever.....................63

Take my Time!.....................64

Kind of Love 65

I didn't know 66

Sex With Me 68

Only if 69

She said 70

Strokes 72

The Moments of My Soul 74

A Love Song 75

This Love Thing 77

Silhouette 79

Here I am 80

Have you ever 81

Free to love 82

I can't stop 83

When I 84

I Can't Wait 85

The sweetest Love 87

The Purest of Hearts 88

Just ride with me 89

Unbreakable 90

The Sweetest Nectar 91

Specifically for you 93

Why can't I 95

Could you imagine 97

What was it 98

If only 99

I'm with you 100

I can't 101

When I see you 102

Can You 103

On this day 104

My Imagination 105

You don't have to 106

Don't let it be 107

She does it for me 108

True Love 109

Elation 110

I'm sorry 111

Especially for you 113

When l 115

A Vibe 116

Insecure Thoughts 117

If only you knew 119

Doubts 120

Unwrapped 121

Consumption of You 123

Open Your Eyes 125

Wait 126

Facts 127

But Us 129

My SoulMate 131

My Love 132

The other part of me 133

F.A.F.O. 134

THE FINALE 137

You Porn for tonight 138

The Heart of a Man, His Unapologetic Poetic Expressions will take you on a journey through time that will awaken experiences in your life's journey, tapping into your love languages, driving your emotions, and setting your soul on fire; for his words will challenge your mind and thoughts while at the same time restoring the power of living life with a new perspective for love and satisfaction. Regardless of your gender, this book will help you feel the warmth of love, bath in the comfort of passion, and kiss the fragrance of your own sexual desires while also helping you to heal through past experiences.

The author demonstrates signs of celebrating freedom and expression after the pain. To unfold this book, a remarkable human experience through the lens of an educator, has been a remarkable opportunity. While reading, the humanistic side of me gravitated to making a connection with the Social Emotional welfare of humans and the importance of expression, whether it be happiness of sadness. It is a pleasure to see a male author express and be expressive of his emotions because so often, the male gender will not, but instead will suppress his thoughts and feelings, leading to, in some cases, self and relationship destruction.

While this book is written through the art of poetic expression. The direction of thought leads down multiple paths, providing light to even the darkest of journeys. In conclusion, I personally believe the best tool for an individual to heal and or grow is to journal by placing his or her thoughts on paper, as a form of therapy. In this case, we see joy and healing through the lens of a man in true written form. How incredible!

Furthermore, without reservation, I recommend this book as a means of living your best life after the pain. Press forward, Mr. Duncan, and I'll toast to that!

Best,

Dr. Roberta Grace

Life Long Educator

Giving Me

What else can I give if I'm all I got, which says a lot or maybe not depending on who you ask and if they grasp the fullness of me but you see, there is more to this story, and glory you see daily has to be recalculated hourly if not by the minute for once I give there is nothing remaining unless you give me back and this refund called me is more than appreciative to receive back what was once considered a priceless piece but now just the average at least that was your calculation and this creation of distance further confirms my resistance to come back for more because the lack of your presence even when you're present solidifies my decision and my reason to change like the season and move on to move forward but I do thank you.

Last Time I Checked

Not once did I look in the mirror to see my own reflection and take it as direction, more of a deflection of my true self, so self-sabotage I would, and even if I could, I would stay that course with no remorse until that situation ended and never mended my broken pieces became non-repairable.

Last time I checked, the woman I loved the most became a beloved angel as, a ghost to watch over me and cover me; even until now and then she still comes to me in dreams as my tears wet my pillow and I awake for sake of life to see another day that my God has made and slade he did all the demons in my path.

Last time I checked, I was dealt a blow from below my core as if the door to life had closed as I dozed off only to be awaken to call that my womb partner, my twin brother, had departed this side, now my ride of life will be alone and gone was my mind as it wrapped around his nonexistence as my persistence to understand why he left me, however, gifted me the understanding of forgiveness of myself even in death he still resides with me.

Last Time I Checked, I recollected that my granny was selected to join the heavenly choir and be admired by the father who created her and stir up my soul she did when they closed the lid of her casket as I became a basket case for all my dreams at that point were laced with uncertainty but certain I was of her words of encouragement for they have kept me sane and remain in my existence.

Last Time I Checked, I've finally arrived as I've survived my own disaster and became the master of my own fate as I still struggle to relate for the gates of my own desires open up and show me who I really am and I be dammed if I go back to who I once was.

Sprinkle

Refreshing is the feel when it reaches your skin, calming the spirit as if lifting burdens that weigh you down.

Just a little here and there, which finds its way everywhere all over me, and the glee experienced in the moment is felt for a lifetime, and for no rhyme or reason, you have sprinkled me with you.

Your love sprinkled over my heart to start beats that tremble my soul to its core, restoring life as I've never known it.

Your body sprinkles over mine, and intertwined we become for the sum of two are now one as a connection with the directed frequency of enhanced joy and pleasure that could never be measured, just treasured.

Sprinkle me now, Sprinkle me later, Sprinkle me forever as I endeavor your wetness as a request, never a test of the unknown, for we have shown goodness to each other everlasting.

It Ain't Heavy

See, one thing about my shoulders they were built for this, even the ones before me proved it, so I'm not new to this. It's just some men refuse to use their God given gift to lift and carry the load because it ain't heavy

Let me take your cares and treat them like stairs, taking one step at a time, never losing my balance for you are behind me to remind me, but any other time you are beside me to help guide me, so don't ever think you are taking the back seat, it's we have a war to win, so I stand in front and your honor I will defend, of course you will do the same and I will accept nothing less, but this one I got so take your rest. You've carried this load long enough, this road called life can, at times be that rough.

So let me take off your shoes and massage your feet, let me carry this load for every step seems weak, however, the stronger I become, even in the most trying of times, my body becomes numb as I revert back to the pain and no shame shows on my face just the sweat on my brow for bend I will but breaking will never be an option. So let me carry the load and lift this heavy weight off yours, my shoulders were built for this not yours

Reflection

Further direction needed as if you've pleaded with yourself not to see yourself for who you really are. Reflection on the year as it's not the past; however, the memories made, the conversations had that bring life back as if full circle, only to start again at the beginning, no spinning wheels more of full speed ahead, so let's press the gas and kick up some dust to thrust into the newest dimension of us.

Reflecting on moments so full of our vide and even the Uber ride was just as much an adventure for your touch and holding you near, the look in your eyes, there is no fear for you have found your safe place in me, comfort and joy with me.

Reflecting back on your Damm near closed eyes as you fight off slumber and surprise yourself with a quick burst of energy that is just as quick depleted and repeat it you do, words, statements that only you know what they mean, I just simply lean in and listen closely with a grin and a smile and the whole while I want to laugh but grasp hold of my Intentions for they are always well with you.

Reflecting back to those moments of connection and my own erections reach points of perfection as I enter your paradise and I get a chance to lick on my piece, my slice of something so delicious that only the finest and the best of the best can attest to its uniqueNess for its exquisite.

So let's continue to reflect always for the days of old can be turned to the days of new, it's us that direct that path daily.

The Soul of A Man

Sculptured in the image of the one who created me and my every fiber is a reflection of his glory as I tell this story of a Soul of Man and expand on questions asked giving answers that may cause confusion for an illusion it's not.

The Soul of Man is seated deep in his personality where reality resides but is most times hidden for forbidden fruit partaken has shaken his being so therefore seeing clearly becomes a blur and clouded is his judgment for he remembers not that his footsteps are guided by the one who created him.

The Soul of A Man, this Man that stands before you, adores you, not for who you were but who you are, and even your scars give instruction to the deepest parts of your soul as I consider my own.

This Man understands and knows that his foundation was formed and created just for him as his will demonstrates a fortitude that can conquer any unsettling desire for that fire is only a temporary flame that can weaken even the strongest man, however, his intellectual ability provides the facility to meditate and facilitate a meaningful emotional solution, bringing mind, body, and soul back to center.

She Arrived

No advance notification given, just some advice taken as she took a risk to exist in my presence, and even with the absence of emotion, she still showed up as if devoted to me already.

No preconceived notions made, just a non-agenda established as we went with a Vibe felt flow that led to a path never taken, as neither of us were shaken, more like taken back to a lack thereof and giving each other genuine attentiveness and eyes being focused solely on us and no force needed just a freeness to be ourselves.

She Arrived and showed me things about myself that life events had not taken away but had become hidden even from my own existence.

She Arrived and gave a new outlook on love as she presented herself as a poem written many moons ago and showed up as words in motion, a perfect picture painted.

She Arrived and allowed me to express the truest part of myself with no judgment made, more of a blank canvas to lay naked on and paint my authentic self.

She Arrived and gave all of herself without resistance and no persistence on my end for the mended parts of her brokenness spoke volumes even in her silence for resilience has taken on a whole new meaning, and the glow on face traced back to glimpses of me as I think of her always even back before her existence.

She Arrived and has thrived in my space, not surviving in space. I'm just glad she Arrived.

Rose Petals

Open the door and, close your eyes, and let me guide you through. Step on this petal and feel how it caresses the bottom of your feet for every step taken I'm aiming to awaken the other side and slide my way in to mend your broken pieces.

Step on this petal for it signifies the butterflies in my gut, and my slut I want you to be this night as I never want to test you but bring out the best in you and let your hue as if dew moisturizing my skin and spin you I will, not like a wheel more like a thrill ride never experienced before and ignore I won't not a single inch of your outer and your inner will soon recognize the same as you call out my name and not in vain.

Step on this petal, but keep your composure, remember you're safe it's just lack of exposure, exposure to a man like me that's intentionally skilled and my will and drive will have you wondering if you will survive this night of pleasure and the treasure in the end will be your new beginning for your head won't stop spinning and your face won't stop glowing for you are showing all the signs of happiness.

Step on this petal and pause for a moment and hear my applause for you and as I give you your flowers with just due, for this you I'm so intrigued, and even if no words spoken, look into my eyes and see that my soul has been awoken to beauty untarnished.

Step on this petal and let it lift you off your feet and land in my arms for I want to hold you for just a little while, then fold you up for a long while, and the whole while, I'm smiling on the inside for joy has overtaken me, never did it shake me for my focus is on you.

Now finally, lay your head on these rose petals and inhale the aroma, and it's not trauma I plan to create. I just want your body to levitate as you feel my erotic eruption of emotional connection as I penetrate your mind with my touch, and the other part is just a byproduct of a dream come true. Just let these rose petals lead you to your heart's desire.

The little things

Do you remember the last time someone thought of you before thinking of themselves?

Do you recall before your mind stalls and draws a blank, and you look like

you're confused because you really can't, a time so special but not really but that person remembered you.

Your likes and dislikes were just the same, for you applied both with the same amount of care, being careful not to get caught in a snare of going against the grain.

So you restrain your thoughts only to fulfill the likes, and the dislikes are put on a shelf only as reminders and its finders keepers because you never disclosed all, you only gave clues but your foundation, just like your patterns told the story.

Do you recall before your mind stalls, all the conversations had, the smiles?

The laughter and the occasional tear from thoughts of losing someone so special that its changes your thoughts to self-preservation and the generation of thoughts that only lead to a destructive personality created in a place of non-reality and everything becomes a fallacy.

Not a fantasy based on reality for this could be just as beautiful as the dream that's seen and felt in the mind, but if this could be transcribed with a pen.

It can become your truthful reality for dreams come true every day, and if it's two that have a similar dream as they scream out to each other, you are my soulmate, and we concentrate and somehow consummate this dreamscape into an oasis of our reality to be each other's fantasyland that spans the galaxies.

Letting the moon and sun be our light and the stars our street lamps on this journey beyond the clouds, beyond rational thinking for we have overcome ourselves and no longer a need to conquer the other for there is freedom in dreaming, and it's a place you're not forced to stay for the very day you stop dreaming as the soulmate, you are separated from the dream and will no longer exist, but the dream continues.

Just like the little things having very little monetary value but priceless to the soul for it lets you know you are thought about and priceless it is, you are dreamed about.

Me Myself and I

To visualize something so compromising and surprising, it is to the outside, but come with me, ride with me on this journey to ecstasy.

This may be graphic dam near pornographic in nature and in mind as we bring 4 into our space never erasing our own existence there, so just stay with me as I hold your hand throughout, and you can scream and moan as loud as you must, just trust I'm here as a participant as well.

First, I want you to meet Me as he rubs your thighs so gently and whispers sweet nastiness in your ear, and let's be clear he's not the average for a beverage will be needed before, during, and after and the chatter you hear in your head will be him for some time to come. So don't worry if your vision at some point becomes blurry, it's just the haze of passion coming over you, causing you to see the three in the room with you.

So while Me is preparing your mind, myself will prepare your body, so let overcoming fear be your motivation, and the penetration of Myself provide the much needed gratification for levitation of your body is taking hold. And hold you shall to all the hands that seem to never stop caressing you, touching you in all the right spots simultaneously and organically your whole body climaxes, and now your mind is on a totally separate axis from your body. You can't take no more is all you say, but your moans and screams speak messages of a dream coming true, and you are finally getting your just due is what Myself hears, and your legs speaks cheers every time they shake. They shake as if a constant vibration is running through your lower body, and your juices provide even more lubrication as if saying friction is miscommunication from his body to yours.

Now, I have been standing over you, waiting for your eyes to focus and your mouth to open. Just relax your jaw and throat muscles and grab hold to I and hold it like it's your own prized possession and teach him a lesson he will never forget as he tries to stand without his knees buckling. So I almost expired as you took him higher than any cloud, and loud were his expressions as they turned you on more than your transgressions turn you off, and off popped his head for you have taken the life out of him, so he perishes back to the dust to be the gem he's always been.

Babe

Eloquently spoken as your lips vibrate to make a sound so pleasing, yet it teases as the vibrations create even more temptation as the manifestation of your body's vibe enters my mind, and I can't help but become intertwined.

For spineless I'm not, but this vibration is creating a stimulation that even relations can't compete with.

As it comes complete with all of you, and I would have it no other way, because even a lifetime would be too short.

Heads or Tails

I keep telling myself that I'm not lost, but I keep tossing this coin called my heart in the air, and it keeps landing on the picture of you, as if planted

and now rooted in my mind, and regardless of how deep I dig, you remain rooted as if you're now part of my foundation, and if I broke up my foundation, I would be breaking myself in pieces.

Can You?

Just imagine him adoring you from a distance, watching your every step, watching your every sway,

Imagine his desire for you to explode on two occasions, watching you come and watching you go.

Just be slow in both directions as the eyes remove every layer to behold a tapered masterpiece that only his mind can conjure up, and up he will be with a longing desire that's only satisfied by you, and the more you give, the move he craves.

Let him solidify this image as your mind makes daydreams turn to night screams.

When you see the desire in his eyes that burn like a fire raging, just know that animal you will never tame.

Only enjoy the ride and let your mind and body be free to accept the gift as it's given.

Addiction

If my addiction was you, would you recommend rehab to clear thoughts of a fairytale love and an endless vibe of tranquility?

If my addiction was you, do I lose my ability to reach back and touch me for my hands are filled with you?

If my addiction was you, what drug would you recommend I digest to regress from considering you my backbone, my go hard or go home, my ride or die, or do I let my heart pulsate in your hands, listen to the beat as it plays tunes saying "Call My Name," can you hear it, most importantly can you feel it.

Yes, I have chosen you my drug of choice, no remorse as I rejoice with visions of you in my minddistance could never separate me from my addiction as it's an affliction I chose to bear, but my addiction, you misperceived as a hindrance and a closure of space, you can't even recognize that you are my drug of choice, my addiction, my affliction.

You are my habit, hard to break, but with your refusal to accept, I have no other choice but to go through this shit called withdrawal.

Does she still exist?

You know, that one with some old school ways and a whole lot of new school flavor, the one with whom the conversation is always on point and the take away you savor.

One whose ways reflect more of things of the past than what she had in the past to bring it to the present, making for a not so certain future, at least for some, because I wonder does she still exist.

One whose virtues are never tainted by what the world does or sees as a trend, she is one of true integrity, and her standards will not be broken, regardless of the outer appearance for nothing she will bend.

One whose words are always with kindness, nothing never said to kill the spirit, only up building and reassurance giving insurance that this triple A policy will never expire but grow in its value with the highest return possible because for this small investment, I promise to make all your dreams come true even the ones not even thought of whether big or small but I still wonder does she still exist?

No fuck yous maybe I want to suck you, as we give in kind satisfaction with the reaction always being one of pleasure, never having to think about the measure of time spent for a moment can last forever, so time limits don't exist even if it's just a kiss to say hello and a good bye is never spoken of more like see you later so good bye is never going to be better for goodbye is forever even spoken of in a letter.

A Couple of Forever's are Not Needed

Fast forward to forever, and tomorrow will cease to exist as the urge to be anxious about the next day will fade, for all days will be filled with unforgettable moments, even if nothing is the agenda - we are.

No cares. For the world is our platter, as we scatter us in every corner only to come back and see we're still there. We are the sand on beaches as they reach shore-to-shore and the more you spread it out, it still finds a way of coming back together, because we do have forever, and as clever as it seems, the lever called reality has been broken, and the token of love that we grant each other has paid in advance a couple of forever's when one is only needed.

Our lives filled with a never-ending flow of possibilities, and the responsibilities are all to us, as we thrust ourselves overboard to swim in the ocean of each other's mind, for they have become interwoven to make one, and burnt on both ends, creating an inseparable bond, that forever is not enough time to separate.

Silent Night

As the sun passes its midpoint and the day comes to a close, the temperature starts to fall, and now a chill has come over me.

Let us break out the blankets to sit in front of a slow burning fire; the nights just begun no time soon should we tire. Your eyes reflect the flames, and your body glistens from the oils applied shortly before, I kiss you with tenderness, trying to reach your core.

The core of your being is where you let all cares be the past, and the present moment, let's stay here and make it last. Let us make love together with our souls bonded as one, let us make love without sound for your expression will be volume enough.

I will hear your screams, your moans as tones of joy and pleasure and will go silently into the good night, hold each other all through the night as will not be a factor for our love force will stop time in its tracks so we can let our minds run free, from and to each other.

We can be silent yet still understood, as our minds will have conversations about the what ifs, but we stay in the moment. I want something warm, I want something sweet, and I want to take my time with this one, slow and deep.

Extension of Goodness

Reaching heights taller than the highest building, your emotions will be added lubrication as you go on this vacation with me. This extension of goodness opens you up, easing your tension so you can view love making from another dimension.

Let yourself be free as this extension of goodness fills even the deepest void for your walls massage this goodness with goodness. Your hips move as if Caribbean blood flowed through your veins, leading to your safe place as I erase any thought of your past and the last thought you will ever have is me, and this extension of me for we come together but leave separated for my mind is with you and still wanting to be inside you as you release your juices that were once so elusive but the conclusion had been reached just as your climax since the max of my extension is headed in every direction creating a mold of me for acceptance of me for your body will reject any other foreign objects and my objection is not even warranted.

Your mind becomes mine for they are intertwined, and the rewind button is the only one that exist as we find something new and exciting each time for no second is wasted.

Where did y'all come from? Are words often stated for no one has ever given me satisfaction and a consistency guarantee that has no expiration date, only one of fine wine that, with the passing of time gets better, only that you can refill your glass as many times as your heart desires and a reservation is never required. My goodness is extended to you with unconditional love for my rising up is a laying down of you naked exposed as I caress the stress from every limb and limp you are until my extension of goodness awakens your nerve endings as pain of entry is the precursor to pleasure only experienced in a dream.

I embrace you from all angles as you take my mind with every stroke, you scream I moan, I hold, and you try so hard to let go, not of me, but this feeling that's been aroused for miles can't reduce this feeling. The moment I touch you my extension, and not to mention my heartbeat becomes one with yours. I can't get you out of my head or off my head as they have become one, and separation at this moment is not an option.

Wild Thoughts

I can feel you cummin' as your leg muscles tighten, your head starting to jerk, I've only been down here five minutes, and you have just started to receive some of the benefits and none of the perks.

I rub on your breast, holding each just like a Georgia Peach, so juicy and ripe, my type of woman for she wants me inside, but I glide pass like a ship missing its port. I will dock, but not now for these mountains of joy deserve my undivided attention, not to mention the retention of my wants to overpower yours has taken a new hold as I want to mold my d*** inside you, but with great pleasure, I measure my justification as notification to you that I will make you yearn for no one the way you do me, you may be far away but you will still want me, try another, they're still not me.

My attention to detail when talking to you, my attention to your body when it gives me a cue, a cue to head in that direction, and my erection has reached a point of full standing power to last over an hour, shower you with full hip moves to find groves in your spine like mine tilted at angles creating pleasure to your core. I do adore you and only want to satisfy you.

All from my view point.

Because she could

She was reminiscing about that one that woke up her inner beast, and feast he did to say the least, but he left a wounded warrior to fend for herself with Windows to your heart down, seeking a chance for closure, but the exposure was too great to regulate the hormonal imbalance created.

Was it that life had dealt a hand of constant deceit for defeat was not an option? How it is that sweet nothing's become something when actions don't flow as smoothly as that tongue did gliding over your nipples, and the grip of a hand full of ass caused you to gasp as breath became a reaching point that seems far off.

Now, the circles you run trying to chase a Man not wanting to be caught, but you keep running as if relationship training had provided you with a map of his mind that translated into a language only know by him.

Consideration of self-starts to become into focus after a determination that a lost soul not wanting to be found won't be found, so the yearning of your own soul needs attention, not to mention an overhauling to rebuild a heart torn to pieces as it releases pheromones for hunters as you are now considered prey but pray you must to keep your sanity for vanity and selfish right now motives can push you right back on your back as his eyes are closed and yours wide open hoping you would see what he sees and hoping it's you but the shoe being on the other foot he would probably not be in your presence so why are you present in the moment for that's all it is and the second he's done, he's done for no connection no longer exist, and the kiss of fire you so much desire went up in flames when you said he lit your fire.

Stand up and stand firm for your crown awaits you in the not too far off distance, just give it time and space and a whole lot of resistance. Resist your own body and the messages it's sending, a Man can't make you whole, nor can he put you back together or sew up what needs mending. It's your job to figure that out, it's your job to work that out because once it's all out, and you have an empty shell that's you.

Just want you to KNOW

The more time in your presence, I see the need for more time in the present, the present moment of making your day as you always make mine, a kiss and smile on entry and the exits are no different, just we see no need to separate creating distance, not of hearts but of body's being connected.

I care more now than I did before, I share more now than I did before, and I closed the door on the past and opened the window of opportunity to love and share love more than I did before.

I opened the door to shed tears of joy when men aren't supposed to cry, I opened the door to compassion and truth and hide from you no lie. A deceptive spirit has walked out the door leaving honor and manhood behind, and they both closed and sealed shut, leaving me here as I am. I broke my walls down piece by piece, brick by brick only to use them to form a solid foundation, with the formation of us in mind.

If you are not here, no regrets and no go backs, only looking back to see how far back you are, hoping you will catch up soon, for life has not slowed down, only moving faster, thought you would not let temporary temptation be your demise and cause such a disaster.

With choices made and the past being where it is, no reason to speculate on the what ifs but focus on the possibilities, we find ourselves here in this moment, looking into each other's eyes, not wanting to let go because you fulfill my needs without needed justification or notification.

You give assurances reassuring your loyalty, you bring out the me in me resulting in miles of smiles and the occasional tear. As I shed that tear, no weakness introduced but a man displayed with vulnerabilities and insecurities so often not heard but transformed into showy renditions of fake strength when strength and truth are exemplified in that watery substance rolling down my face. As you wipe my face, remember you saw me.

Need You vs Want You!

That magical line of distinguishing the difference between a want and a need. I need you in my life, but sometimes I want you out, I need you by my side, but sometimes I want you to step back. I need you to express your every thought, but at times I want you to keep quiet and listen to the rain drops hit the ground. I need you to care for like me, no other, at the same time, I want you to not baby me as if I'm a child, I'm a grown ass Woman/Man. I need you to be that shoulder I can lean on when times get hard, I want you to be strong enough to remove crutches and let me fall and get up on my own.

I need you to be my number one fan being able to hear your voice over all the others; I want you to be able to handle my success if yours hadn't come yet. I need you to be able to make endless love to me when minutes turn into hours and so on, I do want you to tell me your desire, and I need you to want me as much as I do you. I want to be your knight in shining armor; I need you to be that damsel in distress so I can carry you for a lifetime and eliminate the stress.

I want a life ever after a fairytale come true, I need you by my side to make this come true. A want for more and a need completes it, as I want you more, I need you the same, neither verses the other we treat them both the same. Just understand I want you just as bad as I need you so there's no difference.

From My View Point

Baby, what can I do to put you at ease, maybe a nice long walk in the summer breeze? Ok that's not your intention, that's not the plan, you want to be fucked, made love to is your only command. I can follow your direction just lead me there, I can take it from here, my hands everywhere. Gently massaging your back to release some of that tension. Going to the small of your back paying special attention.

My palms press down, and the small goes in, you say go lower, but it's your voice I can no longer comprehend, I respond to your body as it screams out my name. I like this control thing it's something of a game. Now fast forward to your cheeks, I smack one with love and the other with passion, I kiss both of them twice, she moist wanting an all-night smashin.

I recognize your pain, I refrain, so focused still on your body screaming my name, it's a game I want you to play, but your anticipation of penetration is driving you insane as you scream my name, but I can't comprehend your voice just your body as I find my way lower, as I caress the back of your thighs, you wiggle and move about still screaming my name.

You start giving more direction but correction the path has already been laid. You get out what you put in and soon will be paid. You're still commanding, becoming more demanding, only putting yourself in a more compromising position as you listen to me tell you to shut the fuck up, lay the fuck back as

I make your body talk to itself, wetness between your legs, beads of sweat on your forehead, your eyes roll back, sending your body into a complete state of ecstasy. I am your fantasy come true, I am your tension reliever, and if you're not relieved when I've completed my mission, I will kick my own a** for I did not listen. I have paid more attention to you, more than you have done in a while. I know your inner and outer most spots that make you wild. I can make you cum in minutes or just extend the time out. I touch you with fingertips of fire, climbing from your inner ankle to your inner thigh; you cry and ask why I treat you this way.

Today is your day and the rest of the night too, I will satisfy all your desires and intensify those fires that burn within you. You melt in my mouth as your taste is so sweet, your cl*c so tender I can feel your heart beat. They grow faster and faster as your try to pull away, but my grip so strong I want you to stay.

Be You!

Be You, I know it's not a question or a suggestion you accept, your actions sometimes overstated never overrated by this mass hysteria you sometimes create, but as I relate my thinking to you, I subdue all my thoughts only to you.

Be You without some of that overweight baggage that weighs you down, cut those straps of control, and let me come in, leave the baggage outside so I can come in. Once inside, I will let you be you, scream as loud as you like, just you be you, do what you desire, just you be you.

Hold nothing back for tomorrow may never come, its sooner for most, but for some the day no longer breaks.

Can you imagine you being you without any restrictions, no hesitations, and no reservations? You look and appear at peace, a release has come over you, now cum all over me.

I watch you from a distance, even though close in proximity; your conversion to you is where my interest lies, as I so gently caress your body and those soft brown thighs.

Your cries go unanswered, as a question mark never took hold, your moans a silent sigh, like ice trying to melt on frozen snow. I want you inside out, outside in, you be you and let me come in.

It's Funny

It's funny how you make me smile the whole time I'm with you but frown at times I'm not. It's funny how your voice soothes my soul; my mind and spirit just the same, even lying close to you or just calling your name.

It's funny how when days are long, I long to hear your voice, but silence is only on the horizon, sometimes hot with disappointment, but never that. I want and desire only your voice, your vocals regardless of how dismal, light a fire like no other.

It's funny how I miss you when I just saw you, how I search for you even when you're next to me. It's funny how I sleep and want to hold you close, it's funny how you need me more, but I want you the most. It's funny how the tables sometimes turn, at first it was just lust but now its something I yearn.

I tell you all these things, not as game or playing a part. I tell you these things well-spoken from the heart. Way down deep where passion only sleeps, even further down beneath where my last breath lies, sorrow and pain and nothing but cries. It's at times like these you help make life a breeze, and with you I ease into another chapter.

Would you mind if

Would you mind if I thought about kissing you, caressing you, or just holding you like a little child does a blanket that makes them feel safe and secure.

Would you mind if I went down on you like an eagle stalking its prey, or play with you like my favorite toy, like a boy now a man, my hand, my strong hold grabs you with the gentleness of touch, oh you like that, as you should, I would if I were in your shoes, the news of me coming not to be next to you but lie next to you.

The moans, the screams, why are running, stay, don't move I'm finding my grove, just to prove that you don't mind if I did all these things not falling short of completing your thoughts and reassuring mine.

Confusion and passion sometimes thinking I could treat these two imposters just the same, then your name and your presence bring new dimensions to the chatter that has so often filled the room, but I don't mind even though danger looms. Really, would you mind?

Get Out of My Head

Visual reflections of a silhouette seated just below my eyelid as I try to concentrate on my own reflection for yours becomes intermingled with mine, creating thoughts just focused in the moment, and each time I blink, I see and feel your movement, can't even focus as my feet hit the pavement, almost feels like bereavement because I miss you so much, your presence needed and wanted that much.

You walk into my head as if you own the joint, I ask what are you doing here, what's the point? You say I brought you here and put you there, just like freewill and choice I'll leave at your request so your head can be clear, you keep calling me back to say sit right hear so I can put you with every thought released, always keeping you in mind. Get Out of My head for the bedroom has no place or room for you since you have taken over all other aspects you can't have this one too.

My resistance strong, but this connection is stronger, the thought of making love to you already has me frazzled to the point I have no more fight, only a drive to bring your body into mine to form a mind-blowing bond that transcends our minds and bodies beyond the range of man's comprehension for this dimension surpasses even the rate of blood flow through our bodies. You know what you can stay in my head as long as you protect it as your own.

Love Me Thoughts

You remember the first day of school when you laid your clothes out, the excitement level was almost unbearable, anxiously awaiting the sun to come up. Well, that how I feel with you, so anxious to see your face, see and feel your smile, so anxious to feel your body next to mine, so anxious for our souls to intertwine.

It's a connection made for the movies with you being the star, and I'm just there to support as you amaze me without even trying for you catch me out of the corner of your eye, spying as you gaze into the clouds, looking for that sign when it's right beside you. I catch myself at times going to an oh too familiar place of doubt, am I good enough, am I enough to satisfy your needs and my heart rate starts to speed as I anxiously prepare my mind for the worst and the first burst from your lips are words that can calm any ragging sea you let me know you love me.

Have you ever

Have you ever closed your eyes, and the image you see is my reflection from the moon that peeks under your eye lid, providing light to the darkness?

Have you ever had not one day go by when your presence was the only solace needed and once given it was received as a priceless gift.

Have you ever been told you were the topic of conversation in someone's head, that created a smile that creates envy for the envious, and energy for the ones that feel and see your bright vibes.

Have you ever had words said become action figures moving about the room, creating a fortress for your emotional safe place?

Have you ever given your heart over freely, and it be accepted on bending knee as a decree that it's cherished more than life itself?

Have you ever been put on a pedestal and you keep trying to jump off as if you don't belong, when you do?

Brush Stokes

Brush stokes add beauty to an already flawless specimen, brush stokes give way to all the glow that you hold so dear. Brush strokes release your pains and give gains to confidence, resilience, brilliance, all you, don't hide just provide it to the world as a masterpiece, a work of art, a start nor an ending to beauty unleashed, but brush strokes bring out the radiance in your eyes, the fullness of your cheeks, the voluptuousness of your lips.

Brush strokes compliment your body's curves, creating angles not seen by the eye, but if you close your eyes, you see me for who I really am. I am brush strokes with bristles of sensuality bringing forth reality that I need that brush stroke to comfort me, console me, control me, keep me calm, arouse me, release me from all the day's frustrations.

Brush strokes from your fingertips to the bend in your wrist, the attention to pay to every detail, man, with that brush stroke you have so effortlessly awoken all I have in me. Your brush strokes have given power to the powerless, your brush strokes have given strength to the weak, your brush strokes have not only captured my inner being, but your brush strokes have created a canvas for molding, shaping a Picasso type piece the world has been waiting to see. Your brush strokes have captivated me.

Your smile

If darkness was upon me, your smile would light my pathway, that tender kiss a que that I'm safe, your gentle touch a guide to your safe place. Your smile makes for a long conversation with no words spoken, a lifelong bond with no commitment given or needed as your smile and you being who you are is all that's requested for vested interest stays in the moment not in the future.

Your smile adds life to the lifeless, breath to one seeking fresh air. Your smile is my happiness, never giving sadness a place to stand, no demands made, just some want and desire, once this connection was made it's an ever burning fire. NEVER STOP SMILING!

The Taste of Cognac

Poured over a glass of ice to let it sit and marinate to the state of consumption, making no assumptions about the taste, for its pure like you.

Just as cognac sits in barrels for years being aged to perfection so are you just as deserving to be celebrated when your presence is known to man.

The taste is one, not all can bare, just as your grace, your love, and your care. Your intoxicating ways are taken one sip at a time, savoring ever drop to the point even the ice flows with your every swirl. Just as cognac, you should never be taken for granted, I should never get tired of taking my time with you, consuming your words, and getting high from your love.

Just like cognac, you calm my mind and warm my soul, wanting so much of you I lose control. The bottle has a bottom, but your heart knows no end, so I promise not to waste one drop of it as you pour out all I hold, scared and will always defend.

You are woman, and your every fiber should be treated with more care than a thousand-year-old barrel of cognac to be treasured and put on a shelf where all eyes can see.

Your beauty should be admired and cherished beyond your wildest comprehensive, just like watching the finest cognac being poured over ice.

Lastly, I say cheers to you for your strength, your character, and your beauty as we celebrate you today and every day.

Selfless

Outward magnificence being nurtured by inward purity of self, only preserving stages of life for growth. Your smile adds the pleasantries of body oils, leaving your fragrance to be consumed for years to come.

Your caring nature gives natural medication to the sick at heart and mind; and brings life to that which was once given away to sorrow and demise.

Your passion to understand replaces the need to be understood, for your grace explains it all. The innocence of your mind leaves no room for manipulation, only the truth of thoughts. You give the weakest link strength to carryon to a more encouraging tomorrow.

Your clever use of words, quick-witted responses only add to an already beautiful personality. Your love is so intuitive paying attention when attention would normally not be in the present but present you remain, the same you remain, and the love you share is almost insane. I love you being you.

Infinity

Continue this journey with me through clouds of confusion, no illusion but intrusion by others to see and find what we have. Infinity is the time I have set to keep you close to me, or until you decide to stop the clock, but mine has been repaired and indestructible, throwing away the key never to stop ticking, like my heart beats with life, your breath, your presence gives life to my smiles, gives reason for my season, provides sunshine where only darkness lies, provides joy and replaces the cries, provides a hiding place where danger lurks.

Things will never change, but change is inevitable, so with that change, I will bring range, range of motion, and emotion to follow you wherever you are, if not physically, I am always present when needed, and greetings will give the reaction that gains traction to last that much longer, the closer I come to you, the stronger I become from you. Our coexistence on the premise that we are who we are with no misconceptions about the other, whether lover or friend, we will not pretend as we exist together to infinity and being granted eternity we are fraternal twins attached at the hip when you fall I slip but never losing hold of you...

I got you and will never let go, even if you go in another direction, be guided with the type love that we have shown each other, whether friend or lover.

Far reaching to ever touch the stars above, but we can lift each other to heights unknown, to depths never discovered. From those depths is where I discovered your endless flow of love so freely flowing only knowing my hearts desires, creating burning flames and raging fires. Don't let it end.

Dream Chaser

How did you get here, in this place in my head that causes me to think of you, dream of you, and do it all over again? They say dreams reflect restless thoughts as you run back and forth in this place called my head, making your way ever so cautiously to my heart because you know how delicate it is, and you care for it Just as I care for the tender vessel called you, I mean all of you.

My emotionless state has been moved to action and the attraction has gained strength strong enough to move my thoughts to action. I tried to hide myself from you but can't no longer for you have presented a safe place where the only closed doors are structural in nature and should be there, but even those remain open for as far as I can see, there's nothing to hide so I stay to continue this ride and glide in the clouds because your smile lighten even the heaviest load.

I'm not trying to have my emotion put me to sleep as deeply trenched pains, so I tell you my thoughts and fears, and they become few for I entrust what I must, and that's my heart as I think of you, dream of you and do it all over again.

Climax

My words speak through my fingertips, and your hips are the paper, no caper as I would never take from you what you did not want to give freely. See my words comes through my fingertips, and your body is my canvas to create a priceless piece, an everlasting memory of my hands becoming part of you as I reach in to your touch your soul, your core, your innermost places as if on a journey to find treasure and a combination of pleasure but to measure the point of Climax when your eyes have rolled, and your hands have grabbed hold to mine trying to intertwine our minds because yours has become mine. So, did you really Climax?

Open Your Eyes

Just as the body craves, the soul yearns, the ears hear the passion, the eyes create visions, even when you are visualizing a tantalizing sensation that is starting to dominate your thought process, so the less you think, the more you feel, just open your eyes because this shit is real.

Open your eyes so you can not only feel the strokes but see the strokes as if in slow motion, you see every part of my manhood disappear and reappear for you to catch your soul before it grabs hold of me to never go.

And go you must longer than before for the generation of us causes an uncomfortable thrust of my hips into your lips of ecstasy and erect you see I am.

I would never try to cram myself into you for you will want me inside of you, creating pressure to release what you've held back for so long, and your shortness of breath gives life back to you for you almost lost it, just Open your eyes and you will realize you were here with me the whole time.

Facts

As beautiful as a full moon gives the sky its magnificence, so do you provide and give my soul the significance of your love so sweet and tender that I have to render myself mesmerized as if hypnotized, and it comes as no surprise that in your presence I become confused for you're my muse that leads me to these words as an expression of me to you and the clue that I display is my smile as it's filled with rays of sunshine intertwined in your inner as I want to make you the center of my world, not to revolve around but to evolve with as we both expand our knowledge of one to the other.

These facts are never to be doubted but worn as a badge of me, and I live for you and would die for you, never do I want to compete for your love but repeat the words of love in actions and deeds for the seeds of us have been planted and if granted the chance we will continue to grow as one.

No one will ever be able to separate us for we are rooted in a foundation of love so strong that man has a hard time comprehending the beginning for this us was destined, for stars and even the scars we both carry are covered and received with patience and understanding, never a demanding word, just a thank you, and my pleasure is the smile from you inside out.

These facts rang from my soul, and the thought of separation brings desperation as I look for reasons for you to stay, and at the end of the day if my case is not received as truth, I didn't present the facts correctly, and my love was never received properly.

You!

Kissed by the sun, stroked by the moonlight, as you float amongst the stars and grace the heavens with your presence and a present you are. As I take my Time to unwrap you with my mind wrapped around your body and, slowly, I undress your soul with the rest of you in tow and bestow how good and how beautiful it is to be captivated and elated at the same Damm time by your mind's eye.

As you shed tears of pleasure and measure, you can't my strokes as they spark flames of desire to a fire that will never cease to exist for my kiss will ignite passions in fashions never thought about or imagined. Imagine my kiss as you reminisce with the thought of me always on your heart as it begins to cause anxiety with every beat sending out a distress call to my inner being, and seeing us in your presence calms your soul as you mold yourself around me to create oneness of mind, body and spirit.

This You I speak of, I dream of, a visualization of and above all, the true you shows up to show out as I shout out your name not in the public but in the private space in my soul called freedom as I fear nothing as the world becomes my foot stool. You, please keep being you!

I met this woman

Not one day passes without the thought of her smile slowly crossing my mind as it keeps reaching out to grasp and touch that last time. Her fragrance stays with me like my every breath depended on it. Her walk, her sway like watching a masterpiece being drawn right before my eyes, and the skies open up to let me take a glimpse of heaven for I have found it right here on earth.

Paths cross for a reason, and the seasons although they change, my mind and my thoughts have no ending, sending me to wide open spaces to find a way out when there is none. My body craves her even from a distance as the seas part and make a pathway for these two souls to meet again to make memories only dreamed about and so often talked about as fantasy, however, the truth sets reality free to make the impossible possible.

Her head on my chest slowed my breathing and my heartbeats softly in her ear to sooth her soul as a whole, and her body followed as she lay there as if connected to me, so directed I am to put my hips in motion and only thrust with the sound of the ocean as her wetness becomes my weakness and I let my own juices flow to show my appreciation for this woman.

I met this woman, and she left strands of her soul with me to carry back until we meet again.

My Love

My Love, my heart, before I start down this road less traveled, I want to stop, hit the gavel to freeze the world in its tracks as I relax and pour out to you my inner flow and go down deep inside myself to uncover my longing that has made known that it's too strong to be held back and the exact moment it's hard to trace but know that you've graced and blessed me with your presence in my life and the perfect present you are.

No unwrapping needed because for you I've begged and pleaded for prayer, succeeded it did, and my imperfections are no longer hid for you've seen all and know all, and before you, I stand as tall as I did in my covered skin, my weary but unshaken self, for death could not hold back my heart beat for you. Did you know that my heart beats for you, let's out all my deep seeded emotion for you, my devotion to you.

My heart sings for you, all I hear are sweet melodies every time I speak your name, seek your presence, just want to be in your existence. As for my persistence, it won't cease for you and has awaken a beast that's willing and able to release all I have to give, and if need be, I'll borrow some from my fellow man because he'll give to me whole hearted.

So just as these words have departed my heart and ran down into this pen, I find peace and solace knowing my heart has been poured into you.

Ever

Have you ever had a man touch your soul as if it were your body, reaching places only your mind can comprehend in a dream?

Have you ever had a man make love to your mind, and it climax off curiosity the velocity of his words move faster than his hands, and the control of his strokes bring about clarity to words unspoken, so awoken you are to a token, a gem not given to many but wanted and desired by all, so never stall you shall not for he moves in round about ways, sometimes taking days to adore your inner and concludes with seeing your deepest part, not just your heart, not just what's between your thighs for it cries out in hunger and you wonder how could he be among us and suddenly I thrust my everything into you to create a hue of variations, and your temptation to reel me in grows with such passion that you would never ration or forsake advances as they are yours for the taking.

For the making of love provides your mind and body what it's been missing, and reminiscing of Mister becomes your pass time because you have never met a Man like me.

Take my Time!

Effortless vibes subscribe to meaningful conversations and relations that lead down whatever road the heart desires.

Effortless vibes create an erection of connection, and the direction is never known. No plans laid, just a path forward.

Effortless vibes will have you thinking of ways, imagining days that never end but do cease to exist, and even after that first kiss, that first caress, the thought of you laying in my arms, the thought of you naked even though you're dressed.

Effortless vibes create an old soul with a youthful heart, where age is never a factor but factors in experience as a teacher and life lessons as a guide.

Effortless vibes bring pause to overthinking and just live in the moment, and if forever is the moment, so be it and as I see it, It was effortless in the first place.

Kind of Love

Would it be ok if I loved you the way I wanted to, gave you my kind of love as if you are feeding for two. The kind of love that makes even a weekday feel like the weekend. The kind of love they read about and talk about but never see.

The kind of love, where my love, your love, and our love make three the easy way as we can deal each other's hand and have the same outcome if not better, and the letter that we write each other sounds like poetry in motion. The kind of love with transparency so clear that someone watching us from a distance we would appear closer for the eye sees and the mind and body feel the connection and the direction of our hearts run circles around the other.

The kind of love that gives the world a fighting chance, and the romance that you see on a regular is always modified to fit our cups for we overflow one into the other kind of love.

I didn't know

Excited about the encounter, for count, I did the days, hours, even down to the second, and second thoughts never crossed my mind because I was already in the moment. At that moment, I didn't know that the elusive thoughts would become exclusive rights to a front row seat to a show never experienced, and to be the only participant, gave me VIP vibes as I'm here to enjoy the ride as a passenger or driver for I believe in shared intimacy and even the grimace on my face from shark like bits to my mole like nipples triples my arousal as the pain subsides and I give back to you that which was given to me, but yours is more of satisfaction and reaction of the wetness as I witness not just with my eyes but the touch, the feel of an insatiable thirst for pain unmatched as I catch myself in amazement as you scream for more.

I didn't know you could have a full conversation in the moment as my hip movement thrust life into your soul, and the whole of me is caressed gently by the whole of your inside as I glide back and forth, round and round and your voice becomes muffled by a constant flow of deep penetration until my body releases itself and you yourself show gratification as you say I have claimed my place and even though wiped clean my being still remains.

I didn't know your beast within would meet mine

with such tenderness and care that I almost dared to tear down your walls of Noone can come in as I knock at your door of complete satisfaction, you stand on the other side contemplating if this is for real, and after multiple times, the thrill is not only there but has transcended understanding for nothing was demanded only given as you saw and felt that chivalry is not dead but very much alive.

I actually didn't know now I do, and the clues given have been taken to heart as my mind wraps all the conversations into one to draw a beautiful picture of the next time, just like this time, it will be our time, and you will conclude I didn't know either.

Sex With Me

Sex with me is so amazing as you're gazing into the sky to figure out what planet you've arrived on, and I've shown you the undiscovered constellations so we can create our own galaxy and the fallacy that so often exist disappears from a kiss that only my lips can deliver and you discover that I'm not your average lover for I'm your friend that wants to mend all the broken pieces, the lover that's willing to receive all that your body releases.

Sex With Me can be more than a dream as your call out my name and not in my presence for the distance makes your body immune to resistance, and the craving has you slaving, trying to fight off your own thoughts.

Sex With Me is so amazing that you scramble to scramble and dismantle your female parts to disengage as the consistent pulsating has brought you to a different place as you imagined the sex with me being as amazing as I keep my thoughts to myself, not to mention my hands for the demands to satisfy you would prove to be too pleasurable, and the measuring stick you pull out would never measure up.

Only if

Only if the day could start and end with you, and all the in between would be as easy as Sunday morning.

Only if I could feel your touch and you feel mine as if our bodies melt one into the other.

Only if our conversations were endless and mindless would be the effort, and consistency would never have to be questioned, and denial would never be part of our vocabulary.

She said

When we reach that point of connection in which we can longer be called male or female, but seem to be at once both and neither. Now my mind, like yours, took a turn for the worse, and I started to think something was being taken away, not realizing that all was being given as she said what she said and did what she did, which was be completely connected and into me for she had lost who she was and wanted me to do the same for this was and cannot be a game as the mind would have to overcome some serious obstacles and with trueness walls come down without hesitation and the generation of energy between us two is one that releases our minds from subconscious to an almost unconscious state but you still see and feel all that's around you, in you and most importantly what's flowing through you.

It's like the setting of rhythm where the beats sound so different but gracefully combine to create an intoxicating fusion of sounds that send acoustic vibrations through your body, finding all the hollow chambers and creating solo instrumentals as your body sings for me, plays tunes for me as my moans become your background.

This connection cannot be categorized for even specialized instruments can't even measure the energy source as the moisture starts to increase between your thighs, I still hear and feel your cries for help to be released from fear of being hurt, fear of being walked on like dirt, my visual is none of those and never will I expose your heart's pains for I hold them as my own and take ownership.

I would never expose myself, but your desires I have to put on the table to lay them out one by one as each emits an encapsulating essence of appeal that is so undeniable that what was is a question that has now been answered as all manifest on to me for me to see and find my way through you and I come to you and receive you for you, for all of the patient attentiveness has finally paid off.

The range of pleasures we explore open doors to even more, but only with two hands, yours and mine, and at that moment under my eye, all of your imperfections disappear as I frame you up as a myth and make you a Goddess to forever immortalize.

Strokes

Is it the movement of my hips, or do you pay that any attention, or do I mention the strokes that have you talking to folks in tongue and don't forget I have that too, sucking on it as if I'm a titty baby craving more. The strokes of achievement bringing you out of your bereavement, giving life back to you that you thought you lost, so found you have in me the stroke of life, removing strife if only for a moment, however, the movement moves around your mind and body like a carousel, round and round, up and down and if stroked just right listen for the sound.

The sound that, if magnified, could be tied to a sonic boom as you assume yet another position and you feel the strokes begin again as you think your end has arrived, for you have been deprived for so long that your body reaches failure from my stroke.

My ability to nourish your mind and body to have you flourish to your highest peak, and seek you will my stroke, for it has provoked and enraged your wild side to the point that if you exhale, you would be transforming yourself into who you've always wanted to be, the freak in you, you're thinking it would be weak of you to let this side free, so you count to three to reset for this threat of the real you coming out would be too much but it's too much

hold in, for these strokes won't stop coming until I
do.

The Moments of My Soul

A conversation so invigorating that it becomes intoxicating, creating vibes only visualized in a dream, as I scream your name in silence, for it sparks violence in my soul. So hours pass as if the last time was too short, so I try to sort out what was stated for now, the mood is outdated because it's already gone.

So long I do for your kiss, your touch and lean I do on your vibration as if a crutch holding me in place, so trace I do my steps right back to you, and the hours turn to seconds as I get closer to your lips pressing firmly against mine and intertwine, we become again, and I close my eyes to stay in this moment forever.

A Love Song

Melodies play in the background, taking us back to when I first said Hello and a goodbye was not in either of our vocabularies as the conversation kept asking for a Refill of you poured up to the rim and that smile so full of laughter, so I Cherish every minute not wanting to waste a second. Fast forward to the first night, when I said to you, "I'll Make Love To You," and the hesitation led to some reservations as I was already considering this "One in a Million You" that only my eyes could see at that very moment.

I'm a Flirt were words you repeated back to me for I had talked more trash, and all I could hear you saying was Practice What You Preach for I'm your pupil and ready for my lesson of Bumping and Grinding, kissing, sucking, and Slow Winding as 12 play guides you to your conclusion as you climax and I whisper in your ear "Angel of Mine" and your facial features glisten from the moon through the window shade.

For the second maybe third time, we find ourselves Between the Sheets as each time becomes more intense than the last, but how could we Make it Last Forever when a Couple Of Forever's sounds better as our passions Burn Slow as you request I Turn Off The Lights and

Let It Burn, and before we know it, Its Morning as the sunlight sneaks in to wake us to a new day.

That new day dawned with your head on my chest for before you said, Lay Your Head On My Pillow for your resting place is here, your body I want near, and I hear the birds singing a love song I found love on a two way street and at that moment with all the signs You Are My Lady and I want you to be Forever Mine Always and Forever as I Call Your Name for tears of joy and happiness fall from my face as it dawned on me that this is No Ordinary Love For the Best is Yet to Come.

This Love Thing

Engulfed in a sea of emotion, not being about to think about yourself and your own well-being, it's the seeing and being with that Love Thing that makes your heart sing songs only heard from the Gods heavenly choir.

So, this Love Thing you admire more than one of the most valuable pieces of art as you gaze into their eyes, hoping to see your own reflection, but how, with eyes closed and miles of separation, you base it on the feeling that captured your heart from the start.

You base it on the flow of constant vides rippling through one another's souls. You base on experience for your past provides guidance to your next chapter, and the latter are just lessons learned as you burn those bridges, never to cross them again.

This Love Thing will have your heart skipping beats even in your rest, have you going against your own understanding and still giving this love Thing your best. You give the best part of you for the less part of you still makes the whole part of you, and this love thing wants all and stall it never will for once love enters the building, there is no turning back, just a move forward to a destination unknown.

This Love Thing is the first thing I think about when I wake, the last thing that crosses my mind when lay my head down to rest. Dammm, This Love Thing is something else. Happy Birthday once again, and have a wonderfully blessed day/evening...BY Timothy Allen Duncan.

Silhouette

If I don't make you smile, what am I doing? If you cry, can they be tears of joy for to toy with your heart, knowing I wanted no part of it would not be me, but instead I would let you go, let you be free before I jeopardized or even tried to change me.

If I cannot be your weekend at the end of a weekday, providing you with peace of mind and my chest for your head to lay. If my reasons seem long winded, it's because my thoughts have been extended with only you in mind, with you molded so perfectly in my heart, and the words are never meant to sound brash because, by your side, I would dash to if the call out was made.

I grant and give you space and have little to no regard for whereabouts, but in round about ways, you tell me all without saying a word. If you say nothing, your eyes tell it all, you can't look at me long, you look away, and that's where your eyes stall for if they come back, they look through me, not at me, as that's what I'm used to.

And when the used to becomes less apparent, the transparency starts to look more like tinted windows, only being able to see a silhouette of what was, and I'm not used to that. So is the final conclusion, the fact that I need to step back, and would you give me back.

Here I am

On bended knee, broken but not broken, and willing to let my mended self be at your disposal for I'm not disposable, just ready. Here I am with my thoughts so jaded that even a well cut diamond does not have edges as sharp as mine, but my mind stays focused, never losing sight of the slightest change, for I notice all and fall to my own thinking at times but they are all mine at least in my mind.

Here I am not as a competitor for your love or attention, and if there is another dimension you failed to mention, let me push myself away from the table and remain stable in my own mind and heart, to start a new for the glue I thought held us together has lost its bond and I'm beyond the game of winner takes all, for as you see I'm willing to risk it all and surrender all I thought I gained to keep my name and still be worthy in someone else's eyes. Here I am, a lover of you and a hater of anything opposite of a smile on your face.

Have you ever

Have you ever had someone say your name sensually and then sex with someone else your name never sounds the same.

Have you ever came so hard that you never came again you now climax to the point you are now relaxed enough to enjoy the moment for any movement may mess the groove up.

Have you ever been bitten during the moment and become smitten over the one doing the biting and as exciting as it is, it's still hurts.

Have you ever had your world turned upside down and upright again, and you are still confused about your existence.

Have you ever had someone's presence be like a present sent from above as you shove all your memories of the past to the back of your mind where they belong and you still long to go back there.

Have you ever been loved so well that love became your primary language, and you never spoke in tongues that way before, for a door has been opened that will never be opened again.

Have you ever had your heartbeat with butterflies fluttering throughout as you shout out to yourself this cannot be true, but this me that stands in front of you in glee will set your soul free, but that's just me, because you have never.

Free to love

Can a place called your heart be a place of refuge, or is it a temporary storage facility only housing short lived emotions and devotion is never on the radar, or is it the star that shines brightly in your eyes that give clues to the keys to your inner being and seeing first hand that your stance, your foundation only exemplifies what's really underneath and never a beast you are but a creature of habit that sways the same way as years past.

So last, your love does for the ones you hold dearest, and the nearest of distractions only bring you out as your reactions are never reflections of the true you, just a mirror image of the one you've trained over time to trade out love for the daily grind of a conditioned reality when your fallacy can easily lead to the galaxy above where true love exist, just as my kiss so gently falls upon your lips and your hips leave a silhouette of beauty untarnished.

True love is free without material attachment, just as the sky is free to move about the atmosphere with no destination in mind, just movement. Be free to love without reservation, and the revelation that two hearts can become one finally shows its wonderful face to say, you are free to love.

I can't stop

My mind circles around you as my arms embrace you for my strokes have been ordered and deliver I must as the thrust of my hips take dips into your soul and you splash all over me like a river overflowing.

I can't stop envisioning your curves as they move about your body as if every dimension is destiny walking. I can't stop hearing your moans as if tones from a melody so intense that your every breath is taken in as if it were my own, so dialed in I am, and precision is my aim as I penetrate your most sacred place, never separating our entangled souls as we climb this mountain of ecstasy and the wonders we find on the way will stay with us forever for I can't stop and won't stop even if I tried.

When I

When I think of you, you are my sunrise and sunset, my memory once had that I will never forget. You are my morning after, and my night before, you are the combination holder to my closed door.

You are time stood still, you are my dream almost real, you are the base I want to steal. You are my fantasy coming to fruition, you are my last rights, my benediction.

You are my hesitation turned to motion, you are my moisturizer when my body needs lotion. You are my mountain too high, you are Colorado even if I am.

You are my ride or die, my truth be told, and that's no lie. You are my mirror image, a true reflection, you are a journey never taken with no direction. You are my heartbeat racing, you are my choice worth taking regardless of what we're facing.

You are my life, my love, my peace, you are the climax desired while we release. You are my everything, my today and tomorrow, my pain and joy, and sometimes my sorrow.

Yes, when I think of you, You are.

I Can't Wait

As the sun sets and the moon begins to make its presence known and blown away I am for this transition has been in existence since existence was a word. So, just as this transition has a mission to show the contrast between night and day, I stay forever focused on you because I can't wait to.

To first lay my eyes on you as if you're the sparkle in my eye, the beacon for my night, the sunbeam that brings light to the darkest day. To put my arms around and on something magnificent that even the best gift sent would get a reaction, more of a retraction of thoughts as they reach heights of emotion highs, and physical exquisiteness, causing an eruption of the best part to start yet again from the beginning with no ending in site.

To crave you like an addiction explored, a problem ignored, acting as if it's not there as it's expands to an uncontrollable fixture that overtakes you viewpoint just as you have mine, and my body can't wait as my mind hesitates as we want to create and demonstrate an experience beyond the stars, an experience like the sun passing the moon.

What would happen if we assumed they stopped right next to each other, would they appear the same? So no assumptions made for we did stop next to each other, and our worlds did not stop, nor do we look the same, even our names don't flow off our tongues like they did for with this can't wait mindset, we now demonstrate that we can and we will however we won't.

The sweetest Love

Two hearts mended together not from force but reinforced with a cohesive flow of love so sweet, that to see it would be like a fantasy come true and who knew love could look like that and it feels like that and it is like that with the sweetest love.

A love so sweet that you taste it in the air you breathe as you inhale its beauty, being able to visualize and sometimes create an illusion with a conclusion that most can't even comprehend, and in the end, they still can't figure it out however you all have, and it's your bubble you live in for the world would try to negate your path as it no longer reflects the norm but its normal to you as you fall deeper into that sweetest love.

The Purest of Hearts

Amazing how time flies, but rewind it never does for as quickly as we try to fast forward, we have already moved pass that which was most important, so the only thing we can do is look back at what was forgetting about what is. For the Purest of Hearts, time never fades it just cascades and sees all the blessing surrounding you.

Your light never dim, always shining, always making someone else's day to make yours. Always knowing exactly what to say, when to say it, and how to say, so easily wisdom spews out of your pores like blood flowing through the average man's veins. Even your kindred spirit has been passed down to your offspring for your voice will never cease to exist.

Just as the bible speaks so do your words rang true and this you that I've gotten to know again, as you have watched boys become men and yet you always extend your arms to welcome even the long lost child home. You are the true epitome of The Purest of Hearts, so now and forever more I will always give you your flowers while you can yet smell them.

Just ride with me

It feels and looks like your flying when, in actuality, you are falling in love with a penetration of your soul that you have never been able to comprehend as your adrenaline rushes to your secret place.

The pulsating beat of your heart picks up at a pace only your mind can try to slow down because your body has already surrendered and given me full access to undress you first with my eyes, then my hands only to gently graze over the skin exposed, as your senses come alive and survive you will, as this breathtaking experience takes your breath away and only I can breathe life back into you as I slowly but confidently perform to articulate to you through my oral expression as I disturb your inner beast as I feast on your very nectar draining your fluids as you taste like honey, so pollinate I will your flower for the hour has arrived and now our dreams become Reality.

Unbreakable

Fragile is your heart, soft is your body, tender is your spirit, and unbreakable is your soul as I cherish each one, letting them stand alone for one can become mystified and at the same time enlightened by your glow as you shine not to impress only being you and the hue you display gives your complexion a different tone as if you are one of the unfound, never discovered wonders of the world.

So I make it my duty to never be a burden or a chore only to adore your essence as a substance never depleted, a waterfall that calms the rapids, you are an unfiltered diamond, a crowning jewel, you are priceless and nameless you will never be.

For I see you as unbreakable, and never do I take for granted the gentleness you require for that too I admire, sometimes from a far, as your eyes become my beacon, leading me right to you in the darkest of moments.

Your scent and your aroma gives my very soul pause for applause as what's needed and, most importantly, my love for you has been over seeded in your garden of passion and desire as I aspire to reach for the reachable star you sit upon.

The Sweetest Nectar

Words can't express my desire for a dryer I mean wetter destination with a reputation for changing the world, making the world go round, for this crown jewel has caused wars, wrecked cars, left scars on a man's mind knowing it was designed to please.

Just a story untold, is a story never told, so sometimes selling your mouth, not your soul, is an option, however, the impossibility of the two being combined is mind-blowing, for even the all-knowing knew what an ever-flowing river looked like, now I know what it tastes like.

The sweetest of nectar, has one wanting to pollinate the flower of sorts with my tongue as it distorts your vision as the precision of my tongue lay gently against your lips, creating grammatical slips in your otherwise politically correct verbiage as words cease to exist as I kiss and caress her as a separate part of you.

They say wider is not always better, however just as a letter, I want to cover both sides of your story, never leaving out the middle for it releases your inner juices that flow out to me to be received as a gift of gratitude and the multitude of body and facial gestures are only given as servitude to you as I round out your clit as a lit candle with nothing but my tongue being a handle for my hands are occupied to pay homage to the rest of you.

Do you feel the tenderness of my tongue as it glazes over, back and forth, round and round, side to side, and all of a sudden, the rapidness and suction causes a reduction in your spine as your legs shake, your toes contract and at that exact moment you are free to release the beast inside and never hide from me again.

Specifically for you

When the skies opened up, they lowered you down to me, to love and cherish from that day forward, so backwards is not where I want to go. The heavens gave me instruction on how to care for this fragile vessel, letting me know I should always handle you with tenderness, letting my rough, scared hands add just enough resistance to your skin that it removes only the top layer that exposes your true beauty.

I was also given a list of the qualifications required if I aspired to keep you close, and as I drink from your cup a dose of true love daily, the thought of this responsibility brings with it a certain reality that you are no longer a dream but a dream come true.

So, with you here in my heart, I start to experience the unexplainable, and just like today, my expectations are manageable and a trueness I never thought possible is attainable however, the next thought is, is this sustainable, and I quickly realize you are something of Substance. The Substance that starts my day, the Substance that closes out my night, and even when we fight, we fight to keep this love, to keep this love long, to keep this love strong, to ensure this love always surround us as we thrust ourselves into the chapter of our lives, to always strive to be the best version of ourselves, never putting one or the other on shelves to be displayed as stars for we both are.

Even the heavens allow the sun and moon shared time to shine, and for no other reason, I would let you be my sun and moon for just as you light up my life, I become that shining star for the world to see and without you there would be no me. So if my picture painted gives you a vision of the sky above, you will always be able to look above and see me shining and smile you should as you think about how good it feels to be loved and adored and never be taken for granted but granted this option for love is always a choice. Yes, this is specifically for you.

Why can't I

Seamless sensations pass through my flesh as if meshed together like a hand in glove, and above all, I adore your inner even more than your exquisite exterior, having me looking in the mirror glancing over my shoulder, hoping and wishing I could feel your heartbeat as you come even closer to me.

So questions start to form for the norm has been surpassed, and we've raised the bar a thousand times, my rhythm nor my rhyme seem to capture your attention, not to mention, as I've said it before, I adore your inner more than your exquisite nuances that have me pronouncing words, using nouns instead of verbs, and never speaking of my nerves for they have long since expired and retired me to myself to deal with a love they call madness but glad I am to render my mind, body, and soul to you as a whole.

However, why can't I hold you like it was the last day prior to our non-existence, why can't I kiss you and feel your lips caress mine as I slowly undress you with my eyes, why can't I make your body crave me like an addiction conquering your spirit, why can't I let my juices flow into you yours creating a love potion to be used like lotion every time were in each other's presence.

Why can't I view your absence as a void in my soul because that's where you belong and I long and yearn for you like my every breath depended on it. I can't because you won't let me, and it is what it is.

Could you imagine

Visualize the surprise awaiting you as you open your eyes to a brand new day and not just any day, but a brand new day to a brand new start never experienced, however realized and surprised you are at what's taking place.

It's a marathon of love being showered upon you like a waterfall as it covers every inch of you, leaving nothing exposed for even your inner is filled to capacity, so let no one have the audacity to destroy or take away something given you because you asked and were granted this chance to not only glance at but reside at the place called true love, could you imagine that, if so just live exactly that.

What was it

From the first time I saw your face, and traced your smile to be etched in my mind until the moment I saw the same face and smile and the whole while I was releasing my fantasies for they are now reality and the gravitational pull on my heart only pulled me closer.

Even with my eyes closed, I found you, for the universe had set and seen our paths in motion, and the love potion called US could not be denied. Even as days pass, the thought of you still lingered as if you were in my presence, and your departure has always been an afterthought.

However, now think I do and have no clue as to what the future holds, but hold I will to the hope that one day the face and smile I etched in my mind and heart will become our reality for the gravitational pull has me stuck on you when you are defying even the pull as you push away.

If only

Good morning kisses and hugs as the daybreak is fast upon us, and we thrust ourselves into the day as if it's a fire that we know will burn, but we weather the storm only speaking of sweet nothings for the fire cools and feels like sweet heat now. If only our hearts were ours to give, we could move to and live in that peaceful state called us.

If only the connection wasn't so strong that we could maybe break these chains of bondage, but this link is unbreakable, and take I do the fact that a key will never be found to unlock and free this feeling for its surreal and the chills that run up and down my spine are reminders of being entangled not strangled but loving without reservation or hold back. It's not just an if but is.

I'm with you

Ever wonder why the stars align and form a sign like the big dipper and not too far away the little dipper. It's as if our cups runneth over one to the other, and the overflow are all the other stars that surround it.

As you think about it, one star can light up the sky, and that's what you do for me. My galaxy is you.

My planet rotates around yours, keeping the perfect connection in all directions, and so are my erections as they draw me closer to your inner beauty, and our galaxies collide, and we float above the clouds, creating our own world. I'm with you here and beyond.

I can't

Wanted to pull back because you did, however I could keep myself busy enough to keep you off my mind so I can't move forward without you by my side, so I sidestep myself to keep from disrupting my thoughts of you, knowing that the only noise I hear is your heart beating next to mine as if it were mine and my mind can't wrap its head around anything else but that.

I can't imagine not touching you, caressing you, tasting your lips as if they were my favorite fruit, letting the juices run down my chin, and only stopping to taste the juices and my lips detach from yours. I can't stop wanting to be to be in your presence for your absence leaves a void like a hard pill to swallow.

I can't stop my emotions from being wrapped up in yours, for I yearn for that type of connection. I can't stop my pin from spitting out ink onto paper as if this expression of words is my way of saying I can't because I don't want to.

When I see you

Just close your eyes and let me lead you, let me guide you with my voice, knowing at any moment you can open your eyes and find your own way for its a choice, but the moisture you feel between your thighs are only cries my ears hear and the fear in each step is resisted as I kiss your lips gently saying step this way even as you sway for this day you have lowered your wall and did not fall, not like you thought but you will fall for me when I see you.

Can You

Come with me on this journey called us and thoroughly immerse yourself in me as I am in you.

Can you allow me to tear down your wall of fear and endure with me as we set each other free. Can you be by my side and take this ride with me, glide with me, just come inside with me as we explore the unknown and make possible the impossible.

Can you release your mind, body, and soul to me, giving me complete control as I walk with my fingertips all over your body, not really wanting to touch your physical, it's your mental that I crave for your outer I have already become slave to.

Can you always use words to light our pathway, not words to destroy this road under our feet because defeat would be our last words spoken, and life for us would be no more.

Can you just be who you are and leave your limitations behind you, bring your flaws with you, leave your past behind you, bring your genuine love with you, leave and unpack all the ways and things that will never benefit US... Can you do that?

On this day

Today, on this day, I made a choice with no remorse for my decision has been destined and defined, and I also feel inclined to remind you that it's me standing before you, not thinking about how much I adore you and my deep desire to explore every part of you, it's simply I love you and always will.

On this day, I pledge my friendship for you have become my best friend, and no mends needed with anyone else because this self has made a determination, and this creation of us solidifies our bond beyond tears and regrets are only the things we have not done yet.

On this day and going forward, I want to feel and look forward to waking up to you, coming home to you, making love to you, and sometimes just fucking you, for it may be what we both need and desire, just as we are forever inspired to be each other's beginning and never speak of an ending, on this day.

My Imagination

My Imagination is most of the time all over the place, but now it's focused and more deliberate than ever before for the door being your heart is wide open as I take steps to walk through, not having a clue what I'll encounter but what I see and feel from the outside has my insides in an uproar and it's a chore trying to keep myself together.

You are my muse, my inspiration, my final destination for this creation called you has my mind and body wanting to wade in the water deep and catch the first perfect wave to take me out beyond eyesight as I hold tight to just the thought of you bringing me back to safety.

My Imagination, like my strokes, surpass understanding, giving ignorance no room to exist, only my kiss to your lips as they fade one into the other and shutter off all the noise of any onlooker, for they would be takers if the opportunity was presented however we present US.

You don't have to

Finding myself in a special place called your heart puts me in a precarious position for disappointment is not an option, and failure was never on the horizon.

You don't have to tell me how to love you, just show me all the love you have to give, and I will meet you wherever you are giving of my heart and soul, pouring into you as you pour into me.

You don't have to tell me how to caress your body, for it will speak for itself, and your closed eyes are so open that I see pass your outer, only wanting to explore your inner. The softness of your body gives my hands the perfect canvas to paint any picture in my mind's eye, and the sounds coming from your mouth give direction when none are needed but greatly accepted as guidance to your place called paradise.

You don't have to tell me how to make love to you for our conversations have been a road map with no MapQuest needed as the destination has been destined long before we started and guarded I am of all your inner peace because the release of your inner beast is all I desire and the fire that burns will continue as the heat seeps deep down.

Don't let it be

Don't let it be that you close your eyes to wake to darkness created in your own mind and interweave them to the point that you believe what you hear for your eyes can see nothing at all. Don't let it be that your heart becomes so hardened by your past that you let your future pass you by, and the cold shoulder you gave could have been a warm caress, but you dress it as ill intent and are bent on being right in your wrongful conviction of something that could have been as pure as snow flakes falling to the ground, and however, you even drown out that sound trying to related to a past experience that is now only mirroring your present as you let it be.

Don't let it be that your desire and longing be ignored as impure thoughts and feelings for your mind keeps reeling and searching for that feeling again, and all you had to do, was let it be.

Don't let it be that you stop living for you slowly start dying because you won't open the door so sweet love can run in and kiss you on the forehead, and you just stay there in that moment as it goes from seconds to hours, hours to days to the end of your days for you lay there sleep in death but you live on because you lived and didn't let anything pass you by without adoring its individual beauty.

She does it for me

You know that one makes you smile with just her presence. That one that enters a room and her eyes become fixated on you, and you can't help but to return the gesture. The one that makes you feel as if nothing else matters but you, but fuck her over, and it's like you never did. That one that gives all of herself without reservation or hesitation, just some motivation to move closer to her inner beauty.

That one that checks all the boxes without a marker in hand, one that carries more of a load than the average man, however that's not her place as it becomes and is supposed to be mine. That one that satisfies your deepest desire, one that lights the flame and fuels the fire.

She does it for me as it's metaphorically correct, and if I can be direct, she makes me rise and surprised she is as my manhood meets her womanhood, creating a bond everlasting.

She does it for me, bringing intimacy to the forefront and never phased out for it's intriguing at best, and less of it will never get it because she does it for me.

She does it for me with effortless love and affection, and the direction we're headed is elevated at every turn.

True Love

It never cost you a dime, but time is a must, just like a gust of strong winds, it can and will knock you off your feet, even if you sway, stand your ground for truth brings about its trials however, the smiles will be larger than the sun and your glow, you can be compared to the sun for any room you enter, no one wants to exit because of your vibe as you ride the wave of true love.

True love can help you overcome fears that were once obstacles holding you back and lack you never will for the thrill of true love will have you replaying videos and pictures in your mind that no one else sees but you and your true love. Just like conversations starting with laughter and smiles and the whole while you are bursting on the inside from joy and happiness and not because they make you happy but you are happy with their presence and their existence means the world to you.

True love is a color, a picture painted that's nothing short of a masterpiece, and the release of energy from the sight of the trueness gives newness a glimmer of hope, and the present shines bright as before and forever is always in view for the hue from our connection is felt throughout the universe.

Elation

I know you know what my tongue do, but it's my heart that you need to pay attention to.

Have you ever thought about the things I say as a pause to your everyday and now you view me and the world in a totally different way.

Could you keep my secrets yours as if your own and never glance at me differently, even if given the chance. Is there a way to make your heart secure and my insecurities isolate themselves in an unspoken corner for your concerns are mine, and mine yours, not as chores to be taken for granted but Us granting each other access to our sacred place.

Can I mend your brokenness without you uttering a word, it's just my observation as my translation of you leads me to your healed side where I feel secure and endure; you will no more for I hold your core in the depths of my core, and ignore never your deepest emotions as they lay smoothly on my soul like lotion and rub I will all of you in me and let you seep deep into my soul.

If my ways ever become unbearable, just talk to me as if talking to yourself and love me through my pain for its temporary, but this love thing is a life thing that will stand the test of time as I love you, and we love us for a couple of Forevers.

I'm sorry

I wasn't raised the way I've treated you, using words and phrases as if I'm trying to defeat you when in the beginning all I wanted to do was meet you, not where you were but who you were, now its all a blur and not a spur of the moment decision to stir up any mixed emotions or a love potion to fix my words and actions of the past but to make this I'm sorry last until at least you can accept it, not for you but for me because your only wish is to be free. Free to love the way your heart desires, to give of yourself with no explanation needed. Free to experience even when words can't express it, free to be who you are and never address it.

I'm sorry that my ways turned cold like a tormented soul. I'm sorry that my nonchalantNess offended your most expressive side, and I started to hide even the smallest transgression my confession of transgression led to lessons learned that turned to anger and resentment and repent I never could not to you, but my God, so I ask for your forgiveness not to set my soul free but to set yours on a path that leads to daily smiles and continuous joy and even the harshest words won't annoy.

I'm sorry that we were once one, now so far separated that even the smallest thing makes you agitated and elevated you become, now you say you're numb and now in a place of no return, and I get it and would never forget all I may have put you through, just know I never dimmed your light or darkened your hue, it was just two people that didn't have a clue to how to do it, even if we seen it done.

I'm sorry for the last and final as I've forgiven myself, it's time for you to do the same. The crossroads are upon us, and it's time for a different direction, you may not like my choice for it's love, not rejection. At this point and time, I'm choosing me when at one time I was losing me and to see you happy again is my only prayer.

For at the end of the day, we both have to make our own decisions, it still may be hard, even with precision. I'm in love with me now, and I pray and hope you will get there too, you have a beautiful soul who deserves just due. So, at this point, I set you free to see the world from a new point of view and give you the chance to love and be exactly you.

Especially for you

Plausible expectations leading to reasonable doubt, with intentional intentions being at the forefront.

Lessons have given us a foundation that was once broken, now our love fills the cracks of us, creating a bond formidable to the strongest nondestructive material as we materialize into two indestructible bodies forming us as one, and the one presented is love, kindness, and an intentional willingness to desire each other as much as we desire ourselves. Never letting our pass disrupt our present but having a positive Impact on our future for we are two forevers that give life to eternity.

Especially for you I give parts of my soul no one has ever been given privilege to, and even my wrong turns have been right turns to you. My sleepless nights now make my slumber feel like peace on earth. Holding you feels as if you are my security blanket for you wrap me with a sense of security as if in your womb waiting to be presented to the the world as who I really am.

I've waited especially for you to come into my life as a guaranteed commitment given from God himself as his arms wrap us with his guidance, even in chaos, he calms our souls as we console and mold each other into the others most intimate side.

Especially for you, my every thought is you, not as the center of my life but a freshly bloomed flower to be given daily and the care just the same as I Call Your Name as if it's my own, and own I do my sensitive bones for they make me the person presented.

Never will I resent even a fragment of your being for it's you I crave and would slave day and night to ensure you never endure any pain or stress caused by words or actions; even if distractions separate our thoughts, we found our way back to our space and close out all the background noise.

When I

When I look at you, I look beyond myself and reflect on the moment but remain present in our space and erase we do all our fears.

When I close my eyes, I see the silhouette of your whole being, and the power of seeing you in another dimension becomes simplified for I deny nothing to you or for you.

When I shed tears in your presence, distance is never part of the equation, and my vulnerabilities are normalized, never minimized, but super-sized to the point that you know me, acknowledge me, accept me, love me for you show me that you would never expect but require me being Me and US being US.

So when I make plans for US it's a joint decision and a vision we both share, and the cares of the world no longer exist, just our kiss, our touch, and every caress as we undress each other in public's eye and yet we remain clothed to all onlookers as either confusion is felt or words are dealt from the envying mind for they would never be able to wrap their arms nor mind around US.

A Vibe

When l let life do its thing, then this thing called you arrived and took off with me, not as baggage but as Louis Vuitton luggage for it's never left behind but by your side.

So this nostalgic feeling has me reeling even on Instagram, trying to reprogram even my own thoughts for this vibe is creating an atmospheric interruption in my soul.

Can we go back and trace back our own steps into this vibe called us, yes it a must for your presence brings joy, and your absence leaves pain however uncomfortable your scent and taste still remains on the tip of my tongue as I reach for you in my slumber and if your number is ever called you pickup without hesitation as manifestation was my ultimate goal.

You are the bar set, the standard to be met even if doubt seeps in, there is no regret, more of a reset of who you are, the moon shining above or the bright shining star. You have been placed and never to be replaced as my vibe, my peace, my joy everlasting.

You are a whole vibe, and I would subscribe to your channel any day of the week and for the rest of my life.

Insecure Thoughts

My mind wonders and ponders the thought of losing you, maybe to someone or something, however, this ringing sounds like a wake-up call as I lean not to my own understanding of you but to my past as they grab hold of my sensitive side and slide into my reality and create a fallacy that doesn't exist however your kiss, your touch, your words that bring about action that you love me so much, so that's what i clutch hold to, and hold on to for dear life I do, for you are my hue during my darkest times, you are my rhyme, and my reason and knowing this is not just a season but a dream come true and lived out through eyes so clear that the only blur is US passing by others like the speed of light.

And yes, all of this feels and is destiny given as a pathway that has led to this US, and I must remain captivated not by your body as it may transition but my mission to love you unconditionally remains the same.

With no games played, I take your words as actions in motion as they provide lubrication to my joints as I move closer to your soul, not to take it over but to provide and give you a safe place without ever having to retrace your steps back to healing for we will become one in one another, which gives even my insecurities no place to settle but battle I will to keep them at bay, so I look into your eyes, and I know you are my true and safe place at the end of any day, as the night brings comfort and joy and slumber we will as our worries disappear.

If only you knew

Why does time crawl or even stall when not in your presence but move so fast when I am, so I scramble to delay time, and to no avail, I fail and fall back to a perceived lack, and it's not that, but someone that has your back from a distance never conceived however receive I do all the love and affection sending my heart in a totally different direction that I planned, but I stand here before you to tell you, if you only knew. If you only knew that my heart pulsates to a different beat as you defeat all my doubts and fears.

Doubts

Clarification needed at times when the minds eye becomes blurry and clouded by other viewpoints that clearly don't see what I do but wish they did, so hidden agendas are hid like skeletons in one's closet.

Even when doubts bring about pouts of insecurity yelling from the rooftop, it provides an opportunity to view all others opinions as what they are and gaze into your eyes to look deeper than the surface to uncover something so unique, to even speak of it, it would bring doubt to a closed off mind, but to see it up close it's more of a toast to an amazing specimen as men don't see her inner beauty up close, just a physical glimpse and even that is temporary.

Doubt can bring about bouts of emotional warfare that can tear down walls of unconditional love, so to shove doubt to the side and take this ride called us, it becomes a must that I thrust myself wholeheartedly into you.

Unwrapped

Let me take your mind, body and soul on a journey called US to captivate, motivate, hell you may even salivate at the thought as I reach deep to unwrap you.

Look into my eyes as I gaze at your body laying in front of me, fully clothed, however, you feel bare as I stare, making eye contact only with your soul.

Imagine being unveiled to my eyes only, and undraped you are as I slowly, literally, and intentionally disrobe your untarnished body. Time being taken to feel even the blood flow as goes from the top of your head to the balls of your feet and defeated you're not, victorious you will be at the end of this expedition. For just as the sound a tree makes falling in the densest of locations, so will your body reverberate my inner thoughts as they are laid out strategic caresses that my fingertips feel even the tenderness of your lips, which set? That's not for you to decide as I glide my tongue around and in places, creating spaces like voids that I can only fill, and to seek outside of me, even in the moment, would be torment to your being.

Let my touch, my feel resonate in your mind for I live there, not rent free, just a place holder until your legs sit upon my shoulders, whether high or low, a glow will show exactly what my thoughts produced and let lose all your inner juices from paradise, for sacrifice is nothing that your body will render just a release of sorts for your mind, body, and soul to remember.

Unwrapped you are, as you have brought me to the pinnacle of my deepest desires, setting fires of uncontrollable cravings for only you. Even your juices taste like a yearning manifesting inside my manhood, so thrust I must all of me inside your pearly gates and watch I will your body levitate to heights unknown, a new world experience for expressiveness is your body's responsiveness culminate the penetration of our mind, body, and souls unwrapped and tapped out.

Consumption of You

Slow circular motions with no penetration still create a separation of your mind from your body as the utterance of my mouth connects with your place of sacred desire, and your hold being is paused to the applause of onlookers to include, you, yourself, and your alter ego as the slow, quick and gentle licks of my tongue has your body recognizing it's on vulnerabilities and all your control mechanisms have been relinquished to me for I hold the key as if holding the rose as you rise and release and not in a physical form but a the storm called me has come through unexpectedly causing havoc in your soul, causing your eyes to roll back as your release point is surpassed, so the last thing you thought you recollected were previous actions used as distractions.

Just as your impeccable taste has me trying to retrace my tongues path as I meticulously replicate each gentle stroke until you move otherwise. So to culminate the act, I recall the facts... the fact that I made your body twitch and switch gears as if automatic and the exact science can never be recreated for the master never gives away sound advice to the novice, as experience is the best teacher, so even imitation of my vibe will always collide and fail for the semblance of me will never be me, therefore the takeoff may seen the same but land you never will, so a clone of me will never exist, just like my touch, my kiss, my gentleness.

My impression on you, is my expression to you, so if my presence cease to exist in your space, your space will forever have a void because no one else will be able to take you to that place, nor will you allow yourself to go there, because you have been kissed by the sun and dipped in the sea.

Open Your Eyes

Just as the body craves, the soul yearns, the ears hear the passion, the eyes for they create visions, even when you are visualizing a tantalizing sensation that is starting to dominate your thought process, so the less you think, the more you feel, just open your eyes because this shit is real.

Open your eyes so you can not only feel the strokes but see the strokes as if in slow motion you see every part of my manhood disappear and reappear for you to catch your soul before it grabs hold of me to never let go.

And go you must longer than before for the generation of us causes an uncomfortable thrust of my hips into your lips of ecstasy and erect you see I am, I would never try to cram myself into you for you will want me inside of you creating pressure to release what you've held back for so long, and your shortness of breath gives life back to you for you almost lost it, just Open your eyes and you will realize you were here with me the whole time.

Wait

The time has come for you to cum however, the clever side my mind has the other side of my mind divided as I slide it inside and out and wait for your scream as if in a dream, and the kream that covers my manhood glistens from a dimmed lamp shade just beside the bed as you shed all your fears as if clothes and become naked from the outside in.

Wait... just bend over slightly, tilting your head towards me to see and feel my penetration, and let the creation of energy felt flow and glow you will from my will to please and satisfy and the cry I hear as my spear pierce your soul from the other side and you ride me like life has no bounds and the roads we take have not ending. Just Wait.

Facts

As beautiful as a full moon gives the sky its magnificence, so do you provide and give my soul the significance of your love so sweet and tender that I have to render myself mesmerized as if hypnotized, and it comes as no surprise that in your presence I become confused for you're my muse that leads me to these words as an expression of me to you and the clue that I display is my smile as it's filled with rays of sunshine intertwined in your inner as I want to make you the center of my world, not to revolve around but to evolve with as we both expand our knowledge of one to the other.

These facts are never to be doubted but worn as a badge of me, and I live for you and would die for you, never do I want to compete for your love but repeat the words of love in actions and deeds for the seeds of us have been planted and if granted the chance we will continue to grow as one and No one will ever be able to separate us for we are rooted in a foundation of love so strong that man has a hard time comprehending the beginning for this us was destined, for stars and even the scars we both carry are covered and received with patience and understanding, never a demanding word, just a thank you, and my pleasure is the smile from you inside out.

These facts rang from my soul, and the thought of separation brings desperation as I look for reasons for you to stay, at the end of the day, if my case is not received as truth, I didn't present the facts correctly, and my love was never received properly.

But Us

Finding a starting point when the point is Us and where we are, so far apart, different worlds, different spaces, yet our faces remain the same, and the names, if spoken in a different tongue, are understood, and with a solid foundation, we form Us to thrust forward and onward we go with no destination in mind just mindful thoughts as we are each other's muse in dreams, as memories perceived and deceived we will never be as this journey bypasses even the deepest thinker.

Never forsake the moon for the stars as the clouds can cover all, and even though temporary, the contrary heart begins to wonder and ponder over things of the past, stopping US in our tracks as lack of understanding takes hold.

But Us as we talk more and think less about the should have beens and make a mends with our own souls, we become whole, for freedom has a way of grounding even an eagle in flight as the night sheds its darkness, but the moon consumes the sky and provides just enough light to give sight to the blind as our souls gain traction leaving not even a fraction of ourselves behind, so never a need to look back for our view point forward is endless but behind there are limitations to create degradation in our present.

So let Us be who we are and let the stars align, sending signs of trueness for the newness has worn

off, so we turn on and turn into what looks familiar
even in the flesh and mesh two spirits to create one.

My Soul Mate

She is My Ying to my yang, never thought you would be my everything, and yet as I sing your praises, the gaze from your eyes sends these butterflies I have stored away are finally released from their cocoons to spread their wings of beauty to even make the sky appear as a painting from God himself.

She is my twin flame burning as this yearning goes untouched and much is accepted for our two souls have made the proper plans with no demands or questions asked, just an unbreakable bond that goes beyond what anyone may think or thought.

She is My thought in the morning and my dream when I sleep, she is my hip thrust in motion, and it's almost too deep as she screams out my name, and I take the blame for her tears of complete ecstasy as the stars align to bring my soulmate to my existence with no thought of resistance ever crossing my mind, just a intertwining of souls as we mold around each other.

My Love

My Love, my heart, before I start down this road less traveled, I want to stop, hit the gavel to freeze the world in its tracks, as I relax and pour out to you my inner flow, and go down deep inside myself to uncover my longing, that has made known that it's too strong to be held back, and the exact moment it's hard to trace but know that you've graced and blessed me with your presence in my life and the perfect present you are.

No unwrapping needed, because for you I've begged and pleaded for prayer, succeeded it did, and my imperfections are no longer hid, for you've seen all and know all, and before you I stand as tall as I did in my covered skin, my weary but unshaken self, for death could not hold back my heart beat for you. Did you know that my heart beats for you, let's out all my deep seeded emotion for you, my devotion to you.

My heart sings for you, all I hear are sweet melodies every time I speak your name, seek your presence, just want to be in your existence, as for my persistence it won't cease for you and has awaken a beast that's willing and able to release all I have to give and if need be I'll borrow some from my fellow man because he'll give to me wholeheartedly, so just as these words have departed my heart and ran down into this pen I find peace and solace knowing my heart has been poured into you.

The other part of me

The other side, the other part that makes up this complete me, and you can see, feel, and hear me in the shadows as I've tried to hide this side of me.

The other part of me that falls just as quick as I stand however, the fall may be a blow to my ego, so glad that's no longer a factor as I factor in the cost of staying down too long and strong in my foundation, I stand to not only fight another day but for the rest of my life.

The other part of me that would give you the world, and, at the same time, leave you with it to recreate my own again, and make a mends with myself to say it's best to let go and let gone than to hold on and chase something that does not want to be caught, for at that time it's catch and release for the beast you call the other side has been released.

The other part of me that can love you deep, love you into a deep slumber, and you may recall the number of times you called my name, and please don't be ashamed as I reassured you every step of the way, for my love making is an undertaking in and of itself as I give all of myself to you unselfishly.

The other part of me had to feel to heal from all the brokenness of the past in order to represent as the man I am now and in the future.

F.A.F.O

I Fucked Around and Found Out that someone could love me without reservation and resistance to the thought never came to mind for 24 hours was not, is not enough time to express the feelings as it's healing to my soul, that my soul mate fucked around and found me just as I found her to adore her, spoil her, cherish her for we were both lost, now we've found each other as lovers and friends and the mends that we make takes on a totally different meaning and the definition is how we define it.

The taste of her lips leaves me speechless and sleepless I am as I think of the last time as if it were the first time for my mind and body go back there as I stare at her as a work of art and start to fantasize even with her in my presence and to treat her like a present given to me as I unwrap her to explore this reality of perfection in my eyes and the cries you hear in the distance are of joy and peace as I release my past to leave it in place and never trace those steps back.

So, I come to you naked with nothing to hide and make a choice to choose her, and even when my mind thinks we are an illusion, I reject it as an intrusion to my thoughts, they are planted firmly in our future for the present solidifies my thought process for you are and never will be a guess.

Please don't ever doubt my words as they reflect my heart and they come out as trueness for the newness has worn off, so I may speak less, just listen more for even my profanity is a grand stand of my love for you, and never will I subdue or compress my love, for it will boil over and still spill out, now you have Fucked Around and Found Out Too.

Chapter
End
The Finale

You Porn for tonight

Passion eclipsed by my imagination, you're my Porn for the night, so we let the light shine bright on all your sacred places, and not erase this memory but tattoo it on your brain, for I could never explain my thoughts again as I bend your body in ways and still gaze into your eyes as I'm still your protector, it's just I've put on my director's role and scroll down your body as if you're a script reading and memorizing every line as you allow me to cross boundaries only allowed in your mind.

Let your mind be free to experience me like never before as we close this door to open another, for I've become more than your lover. Be my porn for tonight and let my lips gently suck your nipples as if strawberries freshly washed and let the juices flow from the gentleness of my bite, and fight you won't for the temporary pain will be eliminated as it generates arousal at its highest point and I've only just begun for the sun has barely set as you sit on my face and I trace and write out your name with my tongue and hum sweets melodies as your fluids encompass my beard as if a naturally self-absorbing substance that even when I lick my lips I think of you for your juices have become all exclusive in my skin.

Let my hands wrap around your throat and cut off communication, but let meditation and focus on me be your reason for the next breath. It's never a strong hold, more of a slight caress as we mesh our bodies into one.

Let my entry be an exit to any inhibitions you held on to from the past, and let the exhale before I penetrate help you navigate the difference between pain and pleasure and the measure of me reaching the deepest part of you be the key you give over to me for this door has never been opened before and endure you will all of the elusive dreams, moans and screams because tonight you are my porn and I adore your body at least with my oil of choice and the only regret is not making you my porn for the night a long time ago.

www.ingramcontent.com/pod-product-compliance
Lightning Source LLC
Chambersburg PA
CBHW040908010826
48978CB00013BB/1200